PRAISE FOR M. L. BUCHMAN

Tom Clancy fans open to a strong female lead will clamor for more.

— *DRONE*, PUBLISHERS WEEKLY

Superb! Miranda is utterly compelling!

— *BOOKLIST*, STARRED REVIEW

Miranda Chase continues to astound and charm.

— BARB M.

Escape Rating: A. Five Stars! OMG just start with *Drone* and be prepared for a fantastic binge-read!

— READING REALITY

The best military thriller I've read in a very long time. Love the female characters.

— *DRONE*, SHELDON MCARTHUR, FOUNDER OF THE MYSTERY BOOKSTORE, LA

A fabulous soaring thriller.

— *TAKE OVER AT MIDNIGHT,* MIDWEST BOOK
REVIEW

Meticulously researched, hard-hitting, and suspenseful.

— *PURE HEAT,* PUBLISHERS WEEKLY, STARRED
REVIEW

Expert technical details abound, as do realistic military missions with superb imagery that will have readers feeling as if they are right there in the midst and on the edges of their seats.

— *LIGHT UP THE NIGHT,* RT REVIEWS, 4 1/2
STARS

Buchman has catapulted his way to the top tier of my favorite authors.

— FRESH FICTION

Nonstop action that will keep readers on the edge of their seats.

— *TAKE OVER AT MIDNIGHT,* LIBRARY JOURNAL

M L. Buchman's ability to keep the reader right in the middle of the action is amazing.

The only thing you'll ask yourself is, "When does the next one come out?"

The first...of (a) stellar, long-running (military) romantic suspense series.

I knew the books would be good, but I didn't realize how good.

Buchman mixes adrenalin-spiking battles and brusque military jargon with a sensitive approach.

13 times "Top Pick of the Month"

TRICKY DOG GALS

A WHITE HOUSE PROTECTION FORCE STORY

M. L. BUCHMAN

Buchman Bookworks

SIGN UP FOR M. L. BUCHMAN'S NEWSLETTER TODAY

and receive:
Release News
Free Short Stories
a Free Book

Get your free book today. Do it now.
free-book.mlbuchman.com

Other works by M. L. Buchman: *(* - also in audio)*

Other works by M. L. Buchman:

Contemporary Romance (cont)

Love Abroad
Heart of the Cotswolds: England
Path of Love: Cinque Terre, Italy

Where Dreams
Where Dreams are Born
Where Dreams Reside
Where Dreams Are of Christmas*
Where Dreams Unfold
Where Dreams Are Written

Science Fiction / Fantasy

Deities Anonymous
Cookbook from Hell: Reheated
Saviors 101

Single Titles
The Nara Reaction
Monk's Maze
the Me and Elsie Chronicles

Non-Fiction

Strategies for Success
Managing Your Inner Artist/Writer
Estate Planning for Authors*
Character Voice
Narrate and Record Your Own
Audiobook*

Short Story Series by M. L. Buchman:

Romantic Suspense

Delta Force
Th Delta Force Shooters
The Delta Force Warriors

Firehawks
The Firehawks Lookouts
The Firehawks Hotshots
The Firebirds

The Night Stalkers
The Night Stalkers 5D Stories
The Night Stalkers 5E Stories
The Night Stalkers CSAR
The Night Stalkers Wedding Stories

US Coast Guard

White House Protection Force

Contemporary Romance

Eagle Cove

Henderson's Ranch*

Where Dreams

Action-Adventure Thrillers

Dead Chef

Miranda Chase Origin Stories

Science Fiction / Fantasy

Deities Anonymous

Other
The Future Night Stalkers
Single Titles

ABOUT THIS TITLE

*Other than her Secret Service dog **Trixie**, **Bethany Wilson** has never met a woman up to her West Virginian standards.*

*But when she and her matchmaking German shepherd cross paths with another hill-country gal, **Marine Corps Captain Olivia Miller**, she wonders if she's finally met her match.*

They face the ultimate test of their new-found relationship when a terrorist attack goes dangerously wrong. But putting their lives on the line for what they believe, and who they love, only strengthens the deep roots of their shared heritage.

1

———

"Wow! Mighty snappy in your dress blues, Sergeant Bethany."

"Best watch your back there, Sergeant Alex. Trixie here is just a-looking for something to slam to the ground this fine morning." With a simple call of *Fassen* —Trixie spoke German, of course, just like any reasonable German shepherd—she'd have Alex on his ass. The lawn that ran in front of their townhouses was still dew wet, and landing him in it *would* be a perfect start to the day.

"Ooo. So scared." Alex held up his hands in fear.

His great Russian bear dog was still far enough away that Trixie would get to Alex first, even if Valentin really was the size of a small Russian bear.

Ukrainian Ambassador Tanya Larina came up with the massive dog, already in his protective Kevlar vest, trotting beside her. First she offered Bethany the traditional Ukrainian greeting on any meeting of the three-cheek kiss, then slipped a hand around her fiancé's waist.

"Is Alex giving you any troubling, Bethany?"

"Nothing Trixie couldn't jes knock him on his behind for. Not even worth the bother. What do you see in him anyway?" A question she'd made a point of asking whenever Alex was around to overhear.

She and Tanya traded smiles as Alex offered his ritual groan.

Alex Warren was actually her favorite among the other dog handlers. He was funny and his dog was awesome. She'd met the duo before Tanya ever came along, but men weren't what lit the fire for her.

Though if she were to fall for a man, Alex was the best candidate she'd ever run into, but still...nothing. He'd had the standard reaction to her long-legged blondeness. Which she'd managed to ignore until Tanya had knocked the feet out from under both the "guys", Alex and Valentin.

Rather than asking aloud, Tanya just glanced at her uniform and arched an eyebrow.

"Funeral duty out at Arlington."

"Anyone we know?"

"No. A Marine went down saving the life of the French Minister of Foreign Affairs gone out-and-about somewhere unmentionable. Minister's flying in hisself to do his dance, honor the dead, raise a glass o' 'shine in honor of, and all that noise." Because she was feeling a little self-conscious about her formal uniform —she was always happier in her working uniform or battered jeans—Bethany let a bit of her inner West Virginian out. It was always a comfortable bit of home, even if home was never comfortable.

Tanya looked at her strangely but it wouldn't be about that. They often traded Ukrainian for Hillbonics phrases when the three of them, plus two dogs, were sharing a meal or all out together for a morning run.

"Shouldn't a girl like Trixie be wearing a pretty bow for the occasion?" Alex's grin was cut short when Tanya punched his shoulder before Bethany could react.

"Time for me to get to work before Bethany is forced to hurt you." Then she turned to Bethany, "If you ever needing me to hold him down for you, you just do the telling."

Then Alex swept Tanya into his arms. "You're welcome to hold me down anytime!"

Their kiss wasn't friendly barely-past-sunrise light or even newly engaged hot; it was pure romance.

"Gotta get us some of that," she whispered to Trixie as the two of them climbed into her Toyota Corolla for the drive into the office to pick up an official car.

They, too, were loaded up and headed out. She envied Alex his woman, or at least his relationship. She also envied his beautiful Jeep Wrangler Moab, though she wouldn't have gone for the lemon-yellow.

Tanya's wave was more perfunctory than normal.

That's when it hit her. ...*saving the life of the French Minister of Foreign Affairs,* then making a joke. Tanya Larina had been the Assistant Minister of Foreign Affairs for the Ukraine when Alex had saved her life twice during her first visit to DC.

"Shit, Trixie. I really put my foot in a woodchuck hole on that one."

Trixie looked worried at her tone.

"Ready for another exciting day of patrol?" she offered in her best happy squeaky dog voice.

Trixie smiled even though Bethany wasn't feeling it. The big shepherd then stuck her head out the window into the warm March air. DC was leaning into springtime right on schedule. It would still be weeks coming before it reached into the West Virginian hill-and-holler country, but it was here now. She tuned into WMZQ on the radio, and was soon singing along with David Lee Murphy's *Dust on the Bottle.* Fine wine for courtin'...once you cleaned it up a bit.

Like that was gonna happen.

Washington, DC men wanted classy women like Tanya Larina. And classy women like Tanya wanted men a little rough around the edges like Alex. They didn't want rough-around-the-edges dog handlers with a hillbilly accent that kept slipping out every time she was having fun.

But dang it, it was who she was, so Bethany leaned into the chorus, adding a thick hill-country twang. There wasn't a station in DC that played decent bluegrass, meaning she was stuck with country-pop. Trixie was enjoying the wind rush too much to offer her whine of tuneless harmony. Besides, her dog was more of a rock 'n' roll fan. She always laid down a hot rendition on a Rival Sons or Stone Temple Pilots song.

Yeah, more than a little dust on this lady. Even all prettied up in dress blues wasn't going to hide that.

2

Once she reached the Arlington National Cemetery, Bethany tried texting an apology to Tanya— it sounded lame, even to her, but she sent it anyway.

Tanya sent back something that the translator app on her phone insisted was, "ducks have wet backs even on sunny days." She had no idea what it meant, but the fact that Tanya had sent it in Ukrainian was probably a good sign that she hadn't screwed up too much.

They'd known each other less than two months— only a day less than Tanya and Alex had known each other—but Bethany was already closer to her than she was with most women. Bethany's friendships with women never worked out. She was far better at being "one of the guys."

What was the old line? A single man couldn't just be a friend with a single woman? Yeah, she totally had that issue. Maybe that's why she got along so well with

7

Tanya. Tanya was a hundred percent with Alex, which made her completely safe to hang with no matter how nice, friendly, and attractive she was.

The head of the on-site detail gave Bethany a five-finger hand sign. French Minister of Foreign Affairs was five minutes out.

She stuffed her phone away and scanned the area once more. She and Trixie had already swept it once, but the Secret Service taught you to double-down on every bet if there was security involved.

Spring in Arlington National Cemetery was a time of lush green grass and pink buds on the cherry trees. Maples were already going green at the branch tips, and the sun on the birches shone off the white bark so brightly that they looked polished.

No other burials in the area. Was that on purpose? Probably. Looked bad to the families if there were a lot of holes in the ground. Typically seven to eight funerals per day, but each in its own little time slot.

"*Such,*" with the hard German *ch*—seek. She signaled Trixie forward.

Trixie was an ERT dog. Emergency Response Team dogs were specialists in attack and guard—keeping a suspect at bay. But more and more, dogs like Trixie were being cross-trained in explosives detection as well. They weren't up to the standards of the pure sniffers, but they could detect all of the more overt explosives threats.

They set out at an easy trot around the gravesite,

starting at the dug hole with its discreet lowering gear, and slowly circling out.

Not a lot of places to hide here in the sprawling cemetery.

Still, their job was to check it out. So, as they hurried along, she pointed at the bases of trees, trashcans, and gravestones, indicating where Trixie should sniff most carefully while she herself did a visual scan. They circled the larger monuments. They were near none of the buildings. If there was a sniper in one of them, there was nothing she could do about it—not likely though.

The attack on the French Minister had happened during a kidnap attempt in a former-French-colony African war zone. Her role here was more honorary for the Minister, if he even took any notice of her existence. Not that she minded. Secret Service dog handler was a sweet spot on even the worst day. On a day like today it was a pure gift.

There were only four "unknowns" in view among the vast spread of crosses in this section.

A woman stoically setting flowers by a headstone.

A man working along the far verge with a pair of trimmers. He wasn't doing a particularly good job of staying focused on his job. He kept looking toward the gravesite so often that it was a wonder he got anything done.

A soldier six rows over and ten crosses down who

appeared to be emptying a small bag of dirt. "What do you think, Trixie. Soil from the war zone?"

"Soil from the deceased's home. So that he isn't buried so far from his own soil," the fourth person spoke to her.

Before pausing to assess the soldier's actions, she'd been drawing near the fourth unknown—an old man sitting on a bench under a birch tree shining its little heart out.

"That's a right decent thing to be doing."

He nodded. He was well dressed: slacks, worn dress shoes, and a long woolen coat.

Trixie sniffed him carefully.

Not a passing sniff of, "Oh, he's fine." That was all she usually gave people when she was on duty.

But neither did she trigger to some hidden weapon by sitting abruptly: her danger signal.

Bethany glanced up the slope toward the parking area. The honor parade was approaching. The horse-drawn caisson wagon to carry the casket. The crisp honor guard of Marines. Mourners on foot and finally a few cars to the rear for those unable to keep pace with the caisson. Still a minute or so before there'd be anyone coming down to the gravesite.

Bethany let Trixie ease closer.

Again the puzzled sniff, but no definitive reaction.

The old man watched the dog for a long moment, then looked up at her face. His eyes were aged blue, softer than a holler crick flowing lazy in mid-summer.

"Am I dangerous, officer? Your dog seems a mite undecided." There was something about his voice as well.

"She is, which is very unusual."

He waited patiently.

"Would you do me a favor, sir?"

"Iffen I can." And then she had it. His accent was so familiar that it hadn't stood out for her.

"As one West Virginian to another, would you mind either leaving this area now, or staying right here on this bench until after the funeral party departs?"

"I'll be waitin'. I come to watch my granddaughter some."

Bethany glanced around.

"Not here yet. But she a-comin'. Y'all get along now," his nod included Trixie which was thoughtful of him.

Bethany circled around the gravesite then eased casually along the downwind edge of the path as the mourners began walking across the grass from the road.

Trixie sniffed the light morning air as it brushed toward them from those passing, but she didn't twig to a one of them.

The French Minister arrived last. A pair of UD police on Harleys with their lights going, but no sirens, as they led in one of the Service's up-armored Chevy Suburbans. The new eleventh-generation 2500 HD.

She hadn't seen those outside of the leadership motorcades before. Red carpet treatment.

She traded nods with the motorcycle boys.

The Minister was a tall spare man in his fifties but climbed out of the car looking old. He walked with a cane and an awkwardness that said he wasn't used to it. New injury during the attack? By the speed with which his wife hurried around from the other side, that must be the case.

He offered a nod to the Harley boys and her, but nothing for Trixie.

Didn't matter.

Trixie took a sniff and he too passed muster as he hobbled down toward the grave.

The driveway was on a slight rise and offered a good vantage for observing the area. She moved over to stand with the two other officers.

Trixie sat abruptly.

One officer slapped at the wrist of his jacket. "Shouldn't have done my morning's range work in this jacket."

"Told ya," the other officer nudged him. Spent gun powder often triggered a sniffer dog.

Trixie didn't trigger to the second one. They didn't mind when she asked to scan both of their IDs. They checked out, and the first one had range time logged this morning. She returned their IDs, then turned to look down at the ceremony.

In the distance, the lone woman had sat down on

the grass and appeared to be telling the news of the day to the gravestone. The uniformed soldier stood, saluted the grave where he'd scattered the dirt, then walked away. The gardener had given up all pretext of doing his work and simply watched the ceremony; he must be new. The old man remained on his bench.

He was watching the eight pallbearers led by a captain as they lifted the coffin from the flat bed of the caisson. Of the two horses pulling the old wagon-wheeled flat bed, one was ridden by a Marine sergeant. The other was riderless, a symbol for the fallen comrade.

The Marines moved with that perfect precision as if they were one body. Everything so precise, they didn't even bend a little under the load of the coffin.

And the captain who led the detail was a vision. She was tall with dark hair that swept precisely to her jawline—not a strand out of place. Even the heavy dress blue uniform couldn't hide her nice figure. She moved with more than precision, she moved with authority and power. It was hard to look away from her to keep an eye on the other proceedings.

"No band," she whispered to the motorcycle officers to distract herself.

"Bands are only for Chief Warrant 4 or Major and above. The guy was a Master Sergeant."

Still, the Marines handled the coffin as if it contained a four-star general.

Bethany had never actually been witness to a full

funeral. During the bigger affairs, the ones important enough to bring in US and foreign dignitaries, she'd always been patrolling the outer perimeters. It wasn't often that she was reminded of her service's connections to the armed forces, but they were all working in defense of the same country.

Once the coffin was in place and the chaplain had said his piece, the bugler began Taps.

She whispered a quick, "*Stehen*" to Trixie, who stood up on all fours. The three humans saluted while the firing party of seven unleashed the three volleys of a twenty-one-gun salute. Because of her training, Trixie did no more than glance toward the gunfire.

The lone woman at the gravestone flinched with each barrage. The soldier was gone and the gardener still watched from afar.

The old man on the bench hadn't risen to his feet with the mourners, but his right hand was over his heart—outside the funeral, but a part of it nonetheless. It was awfully sweet of him to show the respect due to the fallen.

3

———

ONCE THE FUNERAL HAD DISPERSED AND THE FRENCH Minister was safely tucked back inside his SUV, Bethany released Trixie from duty with a *"Gute Hund"* (Good Dog), and headed down to the old man's bench.

"Thank you, sir, for your respect. No sign of your granddaughter yet?"

"She'll be here any moment," then patted the bench beside him.

She had some time. The funeral had gone off with military precision and her next scheduled patrol wasn't for a couple of hours. There was always a mound of paperwork and reports, but a chance to sit in the spring sunshine was too pleasant an invitation.

Again Trixie sniffed at him carefully, actually tipping her head until one of her giant shepherd ears pointed straight up as if deeply puzzled.

When he reached out to pet her, Bethany

reinforced the "*Gute Hund*" softly. On duty, anyone trying to pet her might be in for a rude shock and a painful bite.

"What part of West VA are you from, dear?"

"Bethany," she wasn't anyone's *dear*. "Up by Gauley Bridge in Fayette County."

He chuckled softly. "Fet County. Mighta known. Stone's throw from us in Fetvull."

"Small world," Fayetteville lay just fifteen miles upriver. His voice was the sound of home. "What brings you all the way up the four-lane to DC?"

He nodded over her shoulder.

The female Marine Corps captain who'd headed the pall bearer detail was striding across the lawn. Still resplendent in her full-dress uniform; she looked even more daunting at close quarters. Not a woman she'd want to meet on a field of battle.

"Hello, Grandpaw. Sorry to keep you waiting, but I wanted to offer the family my personal condolences. He was one of my men, and I wanted them to know he served with immense honor," she leaned down to hug him gently. Her voice was as crisp as her uniform. "Who is your friend?"

As if the Police Secret Service emblazoned on Trixie's Kevlar vest wasn't a giveaway.

Before she could answer, Trixie offered a querulous whine. It was a sound she never made outside of a Beatles retro-sing-along; she wasn't a fan.

"May I?" The captain asked before holding out a

hand. She, of course, would be familiar with the habits of trained protection dogs.

Bethany nodded that Trixie was off duty as the captain removed her white gloves. When she held out a hand, Trixie licked it.

"Well, that's new." Trixie did that for no one except her. Or sometimes Tanya if she had pizza grease on her hand, but not even Alex.

"What's *your* name?" The captain settled into a squat, even knowing to ask the question in a squeaky dog voice. Not many could maintain their dignity while doing that, but this austere Marine didn't shed one iota of her poise. A beautiful Marine Corps officer who was good with dogs was completely outside her experience.

"Trixie," Bethany managed against a tight throat.

The captain looked at her in some surprise, then back at the dog.

"Tricky Dog?" the captain asked.

Trixie's loud bark right in her face evoked an unexpected laugh. It didn't seem like a Marine should have such a bright laugh, or a laugh at all. When Trixie went to lick her face, the captain was quick enough to clamp a hand over her muzzle, pull it down, and place a kiss between the dog's eyes.

Bethany rose slowly to her feet. Something very strange was going on here.

The captain rose as well and held out a hand.

"Captain Olivia Miller at your service." Her

handshake was warm, strong, and had the calluses of a warrior. The tightening of her grasp echoed her assessment of Bethany's own grasp.

"Sergeant Bethany Wilson at yours. What's a-happenin' here?"

"My brother sometimes fosters puppies that are headed into the training pipelines."

Bethany knew that from six months to two years old, dogs were given to carefully vetted volunteers for maturing.

"I met her a few times when I was on leave. I knew her as Tricky—short for Tricky Dog. Hunter will be so pleased that she made it! Did you ever meet her, Grandpaw?"

The old man shook his head. But the familial relation must have been close enough to have bothered Trixie's sense of smell without quite making sense to her.

"Tricky Dog," Bethany didn't even squeak her voice, but her German shepherd looked up at her alertly. "Huh. Somewhere down the line, her name must-a got shifted in the paperwork." And she'd bet she knew exactly where. Lieutenant "Jerk" Jurgen, the head dog trainer for the whole Secret Service, would think that was a funny-as-hell joke to play on one of the few female dog handlers. Next time they were in for refresher training, she might tell Trixie to do more than just knock him on his behind in the wet grass.

She knelt in front of her dog.

"Trix— Tricky Dog," she offered in squeaky voice. Her dog offered another happy bark. "It's gonna take me a bit o' time to be a-switching over your name, girl. Sorry."

"West Virginia," Olivia grinned down at her.

"Gauley Bridge."

She turned to her grandfather. "I definitely need to be spending more time with you, Grandpaw," not a hint of twang in voice, then looked back at Bethany. "You find me the nicest surprises."

4

"A Hokie? No, you can't be." Bethany reached for another beignet. She couldn't stop eating them. The Bayou Bakery might be Deep South rather than West VA, but it was close by the cemetery and wonderful.

"Why not?"

"But Virginia Tech is in a whole other state."

"They also have a great ROTC program. Olivia's smile slid sideways. "Let me guess, you went north."

"I'm an 'Eer and proud to be. I mean how many times do we have to kick your behinds in football to prove just how much better we are?"

"Except our Hokies beat your Mountaineers at all three of the last meetups."

"Record still stands for the 'Eers." Bethany waved away the protest with a little flurry of powdered sugar that had been clinging to her fingertips. Then she had to dust it off her own dress jacket. Powdered sugar would never dare to dust Captain Olivia Miller's perfection.

"I tried to fix her wandering ways," Grandpaw Miller sipped his coffee. "But Olivia was always a headstrong girl who went off on her own path. Always been an 'Eers fan meself since her father played left tackle there. Round goes to you, girl. Kick her behind. Show her she's not the only one like her."

It was an odd request. How many times had Bethany faced that challenge? She came from coal miners. Women were supposed to marry early and make more coal miners. Even as the trade fell off and poverty swept over the hill country, Paw didn't ease his ways. Maw didn't speak about such things when she spoke at all.

When Bethany had made it into West Virginia University on a track-and-field scholarship, Maw had been merely confused; Paw had scoffed. If she'd gone out of state, they might have disowned her. That she was working for the Secret Service was a disgrace, as they weren't fans of the current President. Any explanation that they were a non-partisan Service gained her nothing with Paw. For Maw, it wasn't a *respectable* thing for a girl to be doing a-tall. Paw did like Trixie though, "T'ain't the dog's fault who she works for." (Insult to Bethany fully intended.) But it eased the pain of the obligatory Christmas and Thanksgiving visits—a little.

But Grandpaw Miller egging her on, approving, as

if she was the one to challenge his hard-charging granddaughter?

The gap was too wide to even think about. She got through the days by riding easy—to fit in.

Olivia's voice held no hint of West Virginia. But as she sassed her Grandpaw about his new girlfriend—the man was eighty or more—Bethany knew just by her manners that she was West Virginian to the core.

When they were leaving to go their separate ways, Grandpaw gave Bethany a hug. "Come and go with us."

She almost sniffled. It was the backwards way that a West Virginian said it was time to be leaving but let's go together. More of a welcome than she ever had back in Gauley Bridge.

Olivia also gave her a hug, a real one. Strong, that felt good.

"Have dinner plans?" She whispered.

Bethany could only shake her head.

"Good. I have a unit meeting down at Quantico, but I'll be out by six."

Bethany could only think to nod. They'd already exchanged phone numbers.

5

"WHERE'S YOUR GRANDFATHER?"

But Olivia greeted Tricky first. "Dogs never understand when they aren't greeted first," she squeaked.

It was hard to mind when Olivia offered her a firm hug of greeting afterward as thoughtlessly kind as one of Tanya's triple-kisses.

"The way you looked this morning, I expected we'd be at some steakhouse or fancy place." Bethany was still having trouble adjusting. Out of her uniform, Olivia still seemed larger than life. She wore a tight midnight-blue t-shirt with a small USMC stretched over her left breast, neatly creased slacks, trainers, and a light denim jacket that all looked impossibly stylish.

"Grandpaw's old enough that one outing a day does for him. He's enjoying room service and a Clive Cussler novel. Don't you like Chinese food?"

"Love it. And the owners let Tricky Dog in without a quibble, which was nice." It was a classic Chinese place without an ounce of DC swank. Fake dark wood paneling, red leatherette booth seats, with cheap paper lanterns and a few geometric piecework wood panels hanging from the ceiling. Just a little dark, and a bright red carpet that only a dog would be happy lying on.

Olivia's smile was still startling.

"You look amazing. Just so strong and sure of everything." The words just stumbled out of her.

"Part of being a Marine. But a Secret Service dog," Olivia held up her hands in resignation as she dropped into her seat. "No competing with that."

"Oh, like that's so impressive compared to being a female Marine Corps captain. Combat-qualified no less." Which was one of the rarest breeds of women in the entire US military. The Marines had held out against women in combat until the bitter end.

Olivia's shrug brushed that away.

From the first moment, Tricky Dog had curled up on both of their feet under the table. She was typically almost as standoffish as Alex's Russian bear dog; Caucasian shepherds were notoriously one-person dogs, even if he had adopted Tanya from the first moment.

Tricky Dog was doing the same and it was either charming...or wholly unnerving. Bethany couldn't decide which. Unnerving because it was impossible to not be attracted to Olivia. Unnerving because the chances of Olivia being attracted to her were slim to none.

But the meal started easily with a Tsingtao beer and debate over favorite Chinese dishes. It ranged through how they'd each ended up in their respective services, crossed over that they were within weeks of the same age and had attended any number of inter-high school sporting events together (Midland Trail versus Oak Hill) without once meeting, and how both careers had landed them in Washington, DC.

"My company just rotated Stateside to Quantico for a while."

"Nice break, or does it make you itchy?"

"Last thing any warrior wants is a war. If I trained my whole life and never saw action...well, no such luck. As long as the world is made of more than two people there will always be a stronger group ganging up on a weaker one."

"A kinda dark view." Bethany kept hoping for more cooperation than conflict, even though her whole training was about identifying and defending against perpetrators of violence. But she kept hoping.

Olivia studied her in silence through another chopstick's worth of Pork Foo Yung.

Bethany fooled with her own Twice-cooked Beef with Snow Peas to have something to do.

"Are you always so positive?"

Bethany nodded without looking up. "I try to be. People always tell me that makes me a naive optimist.

But I figure if I help people... Things just come out better somewhere somehow."

"You *are* from West Virginia," Olivia accused her.

"I was done borned that there way," Bethany shot back, heavy on the accent with pride, unsure what point Olivia was making.

"I can't begin to tell you how refreshing that is. I forget about that in the Corps. For all our unit *brotherhood*, it's a damned hard place to remember that you're a woman from Fayette County. Or a woman at all, for that matter, except when they're shoving it in your face as something heinous."

"Maybe you just need youself some remindin' now and then." Bethany wasn't sure why her accent was suddenly front and center but she couldn't seem to switch it off.

"Maybe I do. Maybe more often than now and then." Olivia didn't seem put off by it.

Bethany tried to read her meaning, but Olivia was abruptly focused on gathering escaped bits of rice with her chopsticks.

When they finished and the fortune cookies arrived, they split the bill down the middle, despite the additional plate of raw beef for Tricky curled up under the table.

Bethany looked at her fortune and sighed. "'Tomorrow will be a very lucky day.' There's a generic fortune if ever I heard one."

Olivia held hers up so that she could look at Bethany as she read it.

"'Maybe it will be your lucky night and she'll invite you home.'"

Bethany studied her for long moment. She almost asked if that's what Olivia's fortune really said.

But her steady gaze answered that the question was real.

How had she missed that? Had she missed that? Maybe her conscious brain hadn't gone there. But it was just the two of them, and it had been the most comfortable she'd been with another woman, hell, with another *person* in a long time.

Had the signs of mutual attraction been there? Yes, she supposed they had. Was it still too unlikely to be believed? Ditto.

And did she *want* to take Olivia home? Only if the fates and fairy godmothers had ganged up in her corner. Olivia was beyond wonderful and lovely.

Then she had a funny thought and couldn't help smiling.

"What?" And the tightness in Olivia's tone was the first time this whole evening that she'd revealed she was nervous. Nervous about asking. Nervous about screwing up what had been a great meal.

A great first date?

"Well," Bethany couldn't resist voicing the thought, "must have been a long tour, sailor."

"I'm not a sailor, I'm a Marine." But her smile acknowledged the joke.

"Still." Bethany realized that she'd meant the question more seriously than she'd thought.

Olivia tipped her head one way then the other as if thinking about it, so much like Tricky Dog that Bethany couldn't suppress the giggle.

She imitated the look herself by way of explanation, lolling out her tongue a bit like a dog.

Olivia's wry grimace acknowledged the joke without having to say a word. Nobody, not even Alex, got Bethany's warped sense of humor. Olivia did.

"Actually, it has been a long while." Then Olivia focused on her face and went Marine Corps serious again. "But I don't think that has much to do with what I'm feeling at the moment."

And that made Bethany's decision. She snapped her fingers and Tricky Dog jumped to her feet, jostling the table hard enough to rattle all the dishes and draw the attention of the other patrons. She rose to her own feet and, ignoring the crowd, held out her other hand toward Olivia.

"Come and go with us."

6

THEY MADE IT THROUGH THE FRONT DOOR OF HER townhouse still fully clothed. That was mostly because they'd driven in separate cars. What was more impressive was that Bethany didn't have a fender bender on the way out of pure nerves. It had been a long time since she'd brought anyone home—to any home.

The hill country of southern West Virginia was not a good place for declaring a non-hetero sexual orientation. And a decade ago it had been even worse. University had been a relief...as long as it lasted. She'd quickly become captain of the cross-country running team. Junior year she'd discovered that Tammy, the volleyball team's lead setter, had matching preferences in both sexuality and below-radar visibility.

The good-old-boys world of the Secret Service was shifting...in the offices. Out in the field, she'd found an almost Missouri-level of intolerance. Alex was a pleasant exception, but he was from San Francisco, so it made him almost as much of an outsider as being a woman made her.

Having Olivia in her home was so disconcerting that she briefly felt like a fumbling teen all over again —one who was with a boy for her first-and-last time not because she wanted to be, but because it was what was expected.

"Can I get you a beer or some tea?" She tried to turn for the kitchen but Olivia stopped her with a hand on her waist. A simple touch that sent a flare of heat coursing through her.

"Do you want me here?"

Bethany could only nod.

"Because I can go."

She shook her head, then caught herself. "It's just that you being a Marine Corps captain is a little terrifying. Next I'll turn into a bobble-head girl and do this," and she bobbled her head back and forth.

In mid-bobble, Olivia leaned in and kissed her. Just that simply, her nerves blinked out.

She'd had concerns that Olivia might just be here for the sex. Bethany liked sex, but she didn't ever want it to only be that.

And the moment their lips brushed, the mutual heat was undeniable. It coursed through her with all the power of Tricky Dog springing to the attack—an undeniable flash of purest energy.

Her other concern was that she'd be dealing with the warrior.

Tammy had been a dynamo on the volleyball court, impossibly everywhere at once to make the perfect sets that had led West Virginia University to their best volleyball years on record. She'd been the same way in private. The sex had been wonderful, but she never let Bethany catch her breath until they both collapsed into exhaustion.

Against all expectations, Olivia's kiss was even more tentative than her own. It was the common theme of their entire first night together: a combination of sweet and fun. At the strangest moments, one or the other of them would burst out laughing. The other would join in because it was simply that good.

When they finally spent themselves, they tucked their feet under Tricky Dog who'd hopped up to lie across the foot of the bed, and held each other with no concern for where arms or legs landed as long as they were together.

7

"There's something about a West Virginian woman," Olivia whispered in the pre-dawn dark.

"What? We have dogs with no sense of manners." Living up to her true name, Tricky had taken over more and more of her side of the bed until she and Olivia were sharing a cot-sized area.

Together they shoved at the underside of the covers until Tricky moved back down across the foot of the bed. She could feel Tricky Dog smiling as if she was totally complicit with crowding them so close together, because they didn't move any farther apart once they had the space to do so.

Olivia's gentle tracery over her body didn't arouse so much as it comforted. "You have a wonderful body."

"Marines seem to have a habit of straight talk," Bethany briefly hid her face against Olivia's shoulder.

"Don't stop." She wasn't sure if she was talking about the straight talk or Olivia's wandering touch.

"How did you—" but Olivia's voice cut off and she shook her head.

"What?"

"It will sound stupid."

"Not sure that's possible for a Marine."

Olivia's kiss was more than a thanks, it was an understanding.

"Out with it," Bethany prompted when she still didn't speak.

"How did you do it?"

"Do what?"

Olivia rolled away enough to be staring up at the dark ceiling.

Bethany let her take her time.

"Be a lesbian woman, who's a success in your service, without losing your West Virginian roots? Meeting you, I feel as if I've—voluntarily—lost some huge, important piece of myself. To fit in!" She sounded both angry and impossibly sad.

"Wait? What?" Bethany pushed up onto an elbow to look down at her.

The silhouette of Tricky popped her head up to see what was the matter.

Olivia shied away from her direct look.

"I'm a lesbian?"

Olivia burst out laughing.

What came next had Tricky abandoning the foot of the bed for somewhere less active to sleep.

8

"HEY, BETHANY. MISSED YOU ON THE MORNING RUN. We, uh—" And Alex stumbled to a halt as he focused on Olivia.

Bethany refused to blush.

Tanya stepped past him and did her standard three-cheek-kiss greeting, a little ritual that Bethany had come to enjoy. "You look very...relaxed. It is good," she whispered.

Then she pulled back and greeted Olivia the same way before introducing herself, "Tatyana Ivanova Larina."

"Olivia Miller," she took Tanya's style of greeting right in stride. Yet another thing to like about her.

"She hates her name, by the way," Bethany warned her. "Your life expectancy will increase greatly if you call her Tanya. These are my closest friends in DC. Which means pretty much anywhere."

Tanya laid a hand on her heart and looked like she was ready to cry.

Bethany quickly covered because she'd never meant to say that out loud.

"The one still stumbling over his own feet is Alex Warren, a fellow Foreign Branch dog handler. He's actually sweet in a guy sort of way. And this big boy is Valentin." Valentin actually let Bethany pet him which had only changed recently.

"Uh, hi. Sorry about that." Alex shook Olivia's hand. "I'd just never connected why I wasn't Bethany's type."

"You're male," Olivia said it simply. Bethany now knew that was her Marine Corps-straight form of a tease.

"I am."

She matched Olivia's shrug of *So there you go.* Then they laughed together. It was a completely hill-country gesture.

Alex looked a bit confused, then offered one of his nice smiles anyway.

But Bethany was a bit thrown. She and Olivia were in sync so easily. Like making love this morning. It had been slow and languorous and so very enjoyable. A promise of more with no questions or doubts about the night before. Back in University days, Tammy always was wide-awake in the first two seconds of the alarm clock's ring. She would have them both thoroughly finished off and be in the shower before the snooze ran out. It had been both an invigorating and an exhausting way to start the day.

"What's on the roster for today?" Bethany sidetracked Alex because she wasn't ready for any questions about Olivia. Not even from Tanya.

Alex pulled out his phone. "I pulled protection detail for a meeting between the French Minister of Foreign Affairs and, huh..."

Bethany had her own phone out and was seeing that she had the same meeting.

"And the Ukrainian ambassador," she grinned up at Tanya.

"Yes. You mentioned he was in town. I felt it was a good opportunity to discuss France's position regarding Russian expansionism and what they could do toward eventually closing the Bosporus Straits to the Russian military."

"Your best friend is the Ukrainian ambassador?" Olivia asked softly.

Bethany nodded.

"Oh." Then she whispered softly enough that only Bethany could hear. "And you were scared of *me* last night?"

"Still might be," she whispered back. "Maybe we'll have to get together again tonight to test that out."

Olivia squeezed her hand for just an instant.

Tanya's smile said that even if she couldn't hear their words, she could make a good guess at what was being said.

Alex was still obliviously studying the meeting details.

Olivia turned to Tanya. "I didn't get a chance to speak with him at the funeral. Would you mind very much if I intrude on your meeting?"

While Tanya was saying she'd be welcome... because she'd bet Tanya wanted to check out Olivia some more, Alex mouthed to her.

"At the funeral?" Showing he wasn't being as oblivious as he'd appeared.

Bethany nodded.

Alex gave her a thumbs up, "Almost as good as weddings."

She considered calling on Tricky Dog to take him down, even if Valentin was twice her size and sitting right there.

"If you can give me two minutes to change, I'll ride in with you." Olivia strode over to her car and pulled a suit bag out of the trunk. Bethany tossed her the house keys and half regretted that she wouldn't be there watching. Of course what would inevitably happen next would take far longer than two minutes and then they'd have to shower again—an image which almost made her follow Olivia anyway.

She barely had time to explain about Grandpaw Miller and that Trixie was actually Tricky Dog.

"So, you're a Tricky Dog Gal." Tricky Dog smiled at Alex for using her name. "I like it. It fits you well, Bethany."

She found the serious tone of his compliment surprising, mostly because Alex didn't tend to say things like that. Usually, he treated Bethany just like any fellow dog handler.

She knew that he'd come East from the San Francisco office after she'd been out there on a training session. At first she'd thought it was because of some misguided plan of following her. But Alex had soon made it clear that he'd applied for the transfer because she and then-Trixie had showed him that DC was a cut-above *any* mere field office.

"Tricky Dog Gal. I like it," she smiled back at him.

They were just starting the plan for her revenge on their head trainer who had most likely renamed Tricky to Trixie, when Alex looked over her shoulder and his eyes went wide. It might have been two minutes since Olivia had gone to change, but it wasn't more.

"Holy shit!"

Tanya made a thoughtful hum.

Bethany turned to see the return of the Marine Corps captain. In her uniform, she moved so differently from the woman who'd been in her bed. When she reached the end of the short walkway from the townhouse door, she planted a heel, pivoted precisely ninety degrees, and strode up to them.

"I'm ready." Even her voice sounded different.

"Scared again," Bethany blurted out without meaning to.

Olivia smiled. "Tonight, you can take it off me.

Once we get naked, I reckon that should take care of that problem some." Then her eyes went a little wild. There was no twang, but it was the first time she'd spoken with even a hint of her hill-country roots.

"Hmm," Tanya hummed. "Come, Alex. Before you trip on your feet again." She pushed him toward their Jeep. He almost face-planted when he turned and walked square into Valentin.

Bethany took Olivia's white-gloved hand, partly to prove to herself that she dared to. "About your earlier question. I am who I am. Them as don't like it, can go swim in a pig waller."

Olivia nodded silently, her eyes still a little wide. "And you say *I'm* the strong one?"

"You're...incredible." Which didn't cover a tenth of what Bethany was feeling, but was all she could think to say to the so-perfect Olivia. The way Olivia saw her was startling. Glorious, but very startling.

The Marine Corps captain leaned in to kiss her briefly. "Yes, I feel the same way."

9

"THEY MUST HATE US. THIS SUCKS!" ALEX GROANED AS he walked by her position.

"Yup!" Bethany spared a brief glance over her shoulder toward where the meeting had begun. The four of them—Tanya, Olivia, and the French Minister with his wife—sat inside on a small group of chairs.

Not safely behind the bulwarks of the lovely French Embassy half a mile away.

Not secure inside the steel bars and the dour brick edifice of the Ukrainian Embassy directly across the street.

No, they were sitting together in a Starbucks. Close by the window. Corner location of M and 34th Streets Northwest, meaning maximum traffic exposure to the coffee shop. Also maximizing their protectees exposure to attack.

"Not ours to question why..." Alex strolled down the sidewalk in the opposite direction.

"...ours just to make it happen safely," Bethany finished one of Lieutenant Jurgen's favorite phrases. Unless the protectees were doing something actively stupid, patrols were not allowed to amend the choices of foreign diplomats. They said, "We're doing this." Then it was Foreign Branch's job to keep them safe while they did it. Sometimes that was easy, sometimes hard.

Starbucks should be safe, but that didn't make it any easier to guarantee.

She watched the street: four lanes of stop-and-go traffic, two outer lanes of parking, busy sidewalks, tons of bicycles...and that was just M.

"They definitely hate us," Alex said the next time he and Valentin passed.

They'd both scouted the interior, and now were staying in constant motion to cover both entrances. Alex had ducked across the street and borrowed one of the Ukrainian security guards. He was posted at the 34th Street side door to ask everyone to please use the main entrance. Almost everyone used the one on M Street anyway, so it wasn't much of a burden.

That meant anyone entering the coffee shop had to pass at least one of their dogs, but it didn't help her nerves much.

"So, Tricky Dog Gal, is it serious?" Alex asked as he walked by. She and Tricky Dog were manning the front door. He was doing slow sweeps along the sidewalk, and the traffic whenever it stopped for the red light or early morning congestion.

"Give me a break, Alex," she said the next time he passed. "I met her about twenty hours ago." It only *felt* serious.

"Took me about thirty seconds," he pointed up at the second story of the Ukrainian Embassy then walked on by.

She waited and watched.

He slowed on his next passage long enough to complete a couple of sentences. "All I did was step into some Stalin-era office to meet the protectee for an escort detail. There she was. Drop-dead gorgeous, royally pissed at the world, and Valentin greeting her like a long-lost angel. Maybe it took me a whole minute, but God I loved her sass right from the get-go."

"I love Olivia's gentleness," it just slipped out when he came by again.

"A Marine Corps captain?"

"You have no idea."

"Hell, Bethany, I had no idea you preferred women. Don't go looking for me to suddenly have a clue about anything."

"Deal." And her nerves were back. She hadn't cared about someone this deeply this fast...ever. Not even her first crush on the head cheerleader at Mid Trail High (that she'd thankfully kept to herself).

She and Olivia barely had to speak to understand

each other, but couldn't seem to shut up either. They'd talked mostly about being women of southern West Virginia being out in the world of men; she'd never had anyone to really talk to about that. On *just* their first night together they'd both said things they'd never told anyone. It had been a single night, which meant that it didn't mean anything—even if it felt like it meant everything. And that—

Oh fartleberries! (One of Maw's few curses.) Bethany's feelings were just one gigantic jumble. The worst of it was hope. The hope that there was more there and they weren't already done. It was all too fast, and she knew only time would help, but she wished—

"Alex," she spoke as casually as she could the next time he and Valentin walked past.

"Uh-huh."

"As calmly as you can, call for backup—at least two cars, quiet, no noise or lights."

"Okay," he didn't break his normal stride, which forced an end to their conversation. He turned the corner to check on the Ukrainian guard posted there.

She aligned herself to catch the reflection when a patron swung Starbuck's glass front door. In it, Bethany watched the man leaning casually on the brick corner wall of the embassy across the street.

It was the gardener from Arlington National Cemetery.

10

"Our side door pal's on the alert. He's called two more embassy guards to hold—just inside their front door. Target?" And Alex was gone by again.

On his return from the far end of the building along M Street, she forced herself to make a show of laughing—nothing but two bored dog handlers here. "Man leaning on the corner of the embassy was watching the funeral yesterday. Not good at his job."

Alex chuckled, and looked through the window at Tanya. No, he looked *toward* Tanya, which would offer him the proper reflection to see across the street. Then he continued on his way with a nod that appeared to be to his dog but she knew that he now had the gardener in his sights.

His glance gave her an idea.

Bethany did her best to casually stroll to the window where the protectees were seated. She could barely see them in the dim interior through her own reflection.

She shaded her eyes for a long moment—also the silent military hand sign for "Keep Watch."

Then she lowered her hand, keeping her back carefully toward the false gardener. As her hand traveled out of sight between her chest and the window, she made the sign for a handgun with thumb and forefinger extended from a clenched fist. She only dared do it for an instant, and she couldn't see inside clearly enough to see if Olivia had understood, or even seen the two signs.

Then she returned to her post by the door as if nothing was amiss. When you didn't know where the attack was coming from, the best preparation was to change nothing.

On his next pass, Alex asked, "What's the play, Bethany? You and Tricky Dog have the call."

"I—"

But he'd already passed her.

And then she saw it.

There were completely out of position.

To her left, Alex and Valentin had just reached the next building down the row and were making their turn back.

She stood by the door at the middle of the front facade.

The exposed windows were between her position and the corner.

Less than thirty feet.

But a van was slowing at the corner. As it did, the side door slid open with a bang against the stop.

She didn't need to see the weapons or the black-masked shooters lurking in the shadows to know what was happening.

"Fassen!" Attack!

Tricky Dog didn't need to be told where.

Bethany swung her FN P90 into position to fire into the van as Tricky raced toward the open van door. The angle was already off—the van was past her position. Now she'd be shooting through the metal of the slid-open door and the van's sidewall to hit the shooters inside. That was asking for a lot from a 5.57 mm round. And they were anti-personnel, not armor piercing.

"Aim high!" Alex shouted.

She shot up at the door's tinted window.

It shattered—to reveal steel plate welded inside.

Fire spat out of the guns in the van and into the Starbucks.

Then Bethany saw why Alex had shouted to raise her aim.

Just one bound behind Tricky Gal, Valentin crossed low under her line of fire. As a snarling unit, the two dogs leapt into the van.

The driver hit the gas, but he didn't make it very far. Inside the van there were panicked shouts and gunfire, then the van swerved hard.

Crossing three lanes of traffic without hitting

another vehicle, it jumped the sidewalk and slammed into the face of the Ukrainian Embassy.

Even as she ran toward the van, she glanced behind her.

The big front window was shattered.

The interior was nothing but shadows.

Shadows and screams of terror.

11

————

OLIVIA WOKE TO THE WORST SOUND IN THE WORLD...THE beep of a heart monitor. Six times since making officer she'd had to listen to a heart monitor.

A fading one.

A corporal and a master sergeant during medevac out of Yemen.

Slowing beat by beat.

Three out of the Congo human trafficking mission. And the last just a week ago in Mali; the master sergeant had never even made it onto the bird after saving the French Minister's life. Flatline before they'd even hooked him up.

She waited for the falter.

For the slow fade that said she'd lost another.

But the beat remained steady.

Even.

As regular as her own pulse.

Her *own* pulse?

The monitor ticked up in rate, which she supposed was better than down.

It *was* her own pulse.

It ticked up again.

She was wired up! It was—

No. She was a Marine Corps captain. Panic was not an option.

Once the beeping had steadied again, she risked opening her eyes.

White hospital. Silent television bright near the ceiling with an ad for little girls...goddamn Barbie dolls. The correct angle to be watched from the bed. The correct angle for *her*. She was the one *in* the bed.

Last thing she remembered?

Watching Bethany's shadow, all Olivia had been able to watch of her new lover—a single night of such possibility—cast onto the door's glass.

Then breaking her pattern to peer in through the window at them before returning to the door.

At first she'd been touched at Bethany's need to see her and she felt the same.

Two pulsebeats later, the hard slam of realization kicked in that Bethany hadn't been merely peering in the window at them. She'd been signaling them: *Look out! Shooter!*

But she'd returned to being a shadow by the door. Perhaps as a decoy?

Finally on the alert.

Spotting the van.

Something registering as wrong before it even opened the side door.

Her own belated dive to tackle the Minister out of his chair.

The unspeakable pain of taking the hit and going down. The agony had been beyond obscene.

Tanya's reactions almost as fast as her own, flattening the Minister's wife to the floor beside them.

Down.

Down.

And the heart monitor was picking up speed again. She willed it back into submission.

Her eyes were drifting closed again when she felt a pressure on her hand. Not some lily-white office-life-soft hand like her previous lovers. Strong, callused. A hand you could hold and depend upon.

Her eyes wouldn't stay open, but already she'd know that hand anywhere.

"Bethany," it came out as little more than a whisper.

A kiss as soft as the sunshine color of her hair brushed Olivia's lips. She tasted the salt of tears.

"Sweet," she managed. "How bad?"

"Severed the femoral artery. You got shot in that beautiful behind," again the brush of salty lips. "But they got to you in time. Predicting a full recovery."

"Others?" At least that's what she tried to say.

"They're all fine. Some grazes in the Starbucks

crowd, but nothing serious. Valentin took a round to the shoulder, but he's so big he didn't even notice until after he ripped out the driver's throat. Not serious. Tricky Dog did for one of the shooters and blinded the other. The Ukrainian Embassy guards even grabbed the spotter by the building. French right-wing extremists. Singing like peepers in the holler on the first day of spring."

"Like...to hear...those. With you."

Bethany lay with their cheeks together and whispered close by her ear. "Docs will kick you loose in a few days, but you've got at least a month of recoup."

Past speaking, she nodded.

"Thought maybe you could stay with me and we could get to know each other?"

She managed one final nod before the drugs took her under.

At least she hoped she did.

It gave her something to really look forward to as the steady beat of the heart monitor lulled her back to sleep.

12

"NEVER THOUGHT I'D BE BACK HERE. BUT YOU ASKED ME to take you to my favorite place anywhere. This be it." Bethany stared up at Cathedral Falls. The sixty-foot cascade was one of the tallest in all of West Virginia. "I used to walk ta here whenever I was needin' to get away."

The village of Gauley Bridge lay just a mile downriver from here where the New River joined the Gauley and together they became the Kanawha.

In 1861, after West Virginia broke away from Virginia to join the Union, the Confederate Army blew up the Gauley Bridge. Only a few of the stone buttress supports remained, but the locals still clung to its memory with pride. It was the "big" tourist attraction.

She couldn't care less.

Her family home lay a half mile up the Gauley tributary and she was going nowhere near the place today. Not even into town. She'd think about introducing Olivia to her family some other day—if Olivia even wanted to meet them. Today was about them.

But here? Here she could sit for hours.

"This is the one place I could be myself. Locals almost never come here once they've seen it. Just tourists. When I was sitting here, no one would ask me to be anything for a whole day at a time. Sometimes I'd come when I knew the long walk would leave me only fifteen minutes here. Those minutes were worth the walk both ways."

"And now?" Olivia's voice was little louder than the splashing water.

Bethany faced her. "I've never been more myself than when I'm with you."

"Not quite the first day of spring. We missed the peepers," Olivia sat down carefully on a rock in the sweeping natural amphitheater the falls had carved into the dark sandstone. She rested her cane to one side and slid her hands into her vest pockets, as Bethany sat to the other.

"First of May," Bethany acknowledged. It had taken another surgery and there was still a few months of physical therapy ahead of them, but they'd gotten through it. Together.

Tricky Dog lay across their feet, which was absolutely *her* happy place.

Together they watched the water spill down the

rock face, splashing into the broad pool that was far too public for skinny dipping. When Olivia was more mobile, there were a couple of crane holes back in the hills that they could hike into and jump on in where no one would ever bother them.

"Maybe next year."

"You do realize what you just said." Olivia's amusement ran deep. By now she knew that Bethany often didn't get the implications until after she spoke. "Or are you being Tricky Dog Gal?"

Alex's nickname had become one of Olivia's favorite endearments.

Tricky Dog snuggled even closer on their feet at even the mention of her name, making it a win-win.

"Uh-huh." Bethany did her best to keep her tone enigmatically neutral. This time—for once—she wasn't just blurting something out; she knew exactly what she was saying. Being with Olivia was the best thing that had ever happened to her. Over the weeks there'd been a lot of caretaking and empathetic pain. But there'd also been more joy than her heart knew what to do with.

Their common but unshared background was just a foundation that they'd slowly built upon until the lines between them seemed to blur. When they made love, those lines disappeared completely like swallows playing in the last of the evening light.

She reached down to pet Tricky Dog, apologizing

because she'd been demoted to second place in Bethany's heart.

"When do you go to France?" Now that she was fit for travel, the French wanted to award Olivia the Honour medal of Foreign Affairs. It was like the Congressional Medal of Honor. It was going to be the first time they'd been apart for longer than her own workday in six weeks.

"You mean when do *we* go to France?"

"I saw the official invitation; it said you and *spouse.*"

"It did."

Bethany turned to face her but had forgotten how to speak.

"I know it's asking a lot," Olivia didn't turn from watching the waterfall.

"A flight to France?" Though Bethany knew that wasn't what Olivia meant, it was the only piece she could latch onto at the moment.

"When I'm fit, I'm going to be back in the Corps. It means waiting when I'm on foreign assignments. It means that when I'm in a war zone—"

"Yes."

"No, Bethany. I'm serious, you have to think about this."

"Already did. Yes." She'd thought of little else these last weeks. She wanted... She *needed* to have Olivia Miller in her life.

"But—"

"I didn't want it to seem like I was pushing. My job isn't the safest either. But I knew it had to be here." Bethany waved at the waterfall. Then she found the nerve to reach deep into her pocket and pull out the slim gold band she'd been carrying for almost two weeks. "Nothing fancy. Nothing that would put you at risk if someone somewhere awful saw you wearing it. I wanted to give you a ring you could take with you wherever you deployed."

Without looking away, Olivia pulled her hand out of her pocket and opened it.

When she opened her tight-clenched fist, on her palm lay a thin band of gold almost identical to the one Bethany had selected. "Fancy isn't you. You shine so brightly that no diamond could match it anyway. You've taught me how to get back to my heart."

"You taught me that I had one to begin with." Which had surprised Bethany no end.

"Bigger'n a spotted bass in a fisherman's tall tale," Olivia slipped all the way down into the deep twang that hill folk used when teasing tourists.

And there it was, the reason they truly understood each other. West Virginian women, putting their life at risk for others, and deeming that life be well spent however long it lasted.

They slipped the rings on each other's fingers then clasped hands, four hands together, and sealed it with a kiss.

Turning back to the waterfall, they watched it flow

as it had for a thousand years and as it would for every single spring each time they made it back.

"This changes things some, you know?" Bethany squeezed Olivia's hands in hers.

"Ya think?" Olivia teased her back.

"Yep." With her toe, she nudged Tricky Dog up to sitting.

She wagged her tail as she rested her big muzzle atop their still-clasped hands.

"We three. We now be the Tricky Dog *Gals*, plural-like, iffen you know what I'm mean."

Olivia leaned down to plant a happy kiss between Tricky Dog's eyes, but got her face licked this time because her hands were still trapped in Bethany's.

"I reckon so," and their laughter was brighter than the falling water.

Tricky Dog's happy bark echoed off the walls, sayin' it was so.

OFF THE LEASH (EXCERPT)

IF YOU ENJOYED THAT, YOU'LL LOVE THE NOVELS!

OFF THE LEASH (EXCERPT)

"You're joking."

"Nope. That's his name. And he's yours now."

Sergeant Linda Hamlin wondered quite what it would take to wipe that smile off Lieutenant Jurgen's face. A 120mm round from an M1A1 Abrams Main Battle Tank came to mind.

The kennel master of the US Secret Service's Canine Team was clearly a misogynistic jerk from the top of his polished head to the bottoms of his equally polished boots. She wondered if the shoelaces were polished as well.

Then she looked over at the poor dog sitting hopefully on the concrete kennel floor. His stall had a dog bed three times his size and a water bowl deep enough for him to bathe in. No toys, because toys always came from the handler as a reward. He offered her a sad sigh and a liquid doggy gaze. The kennel even smelled wrong, more of sanitizer than dog. The walls seemed to echo with each bark down the long line of kennels housing the candidate hopefuls for the next addition to the Secret Service's team.

Thor—really?—was a brindle-colored mutt, part who-knew and part no-one-cared. He looked like a cross between an oversized, long-haired schnauzer and a dust mop that someone had spilled dark gray paint on. After mixing in streaks of tawny brown, they'd left one white paw just to make him all the more laughable.

And of course Lieutenant Jerk Jurgen would assign Thor to the first woman on the USSS K-9 team.

Unable to resist, she leaned over far enough to scruff the dog's ears. He was the physical opposite of the sleek and powerful Malinois MWDs—military war dogs—that she'd been handling for the 75th Rangers for the last five years. They twitched with eagerness and nerves. A good MWD was seventy pounds of pure drive—every damn second of the day. If the mild-mannered Thor weighed thirty pounds, she'd be surprised. And he looked like a little girl's best friend who should have a pink bow on his collar.

Jurgen was clearly ex-Marine and would have no respect for the Army. Of course, having been in the Army's Special Operations Forces, she knew better than to respect a Marine.

"We won't let any old swabbie bother us, will we?"

Jurgen snarled—definitely Marine Corps. Swabbie

was slang for a Navy sailor and a Marine always took offense at being lumped in with them no matter how much they belonged. Of course the swabbies took offense at having the Marines lumped with *them*. Too bad there weren't any Navy around so that she could get two for the price of one. Jurgen wouldn't be her boss, so appeasing him wasn't high on her to-do list.

At least she wouldn't need any of the protective bite gear working with Thor. With his stature, he was an explosives detection dog without also being an attack one.

"Where was he trained?" She stood back up to face the beast.

"Private outfit in Montana—some place called Henderson's Ranch. Didn't make their MWD program," his scoff said exactly what he thought the likelihood of any dog outfit in Montana being worthwhile. "They wanted us to try the little runt out."

She'd never heard of a training program in Montana. MWDs all came out of Lackland Air Force Base training. The Secret Service mostly trained their own and they all came from Vohne Liche Kennels in Indiana. Unless... Special Operations Forces dogs were trained by private contractors. She'd worked beside a Delta Force dog for a single month—he'd been incredible.

"Is he trained in English or German?" Most American MWDs were trained in German so that there was no confusion in case a command word happened to be part of a spoken sentence. It also made it harder for any random person on the battlefield to shout something that would confuse the dog.

"German according to his paperwork, but he won't listen to me much in either language."

Might as well give the diminutive Thor a few basic tests. A snap of her fingers and a slap on her thigh had the dog dropping into a smart "heel" position. No need to call out *Fuss*—*by my foot.*

"*Pass auf!*" Guard! She made a pistol with her thumb and forefinger and aimed it at Jurgen as she grabbed her forearm with her other hand—the military hand sign for enemy.

The little dog snarled at Jurgen sharply enough to have him backing out of the kennel. "Goddamn it!"

"*Ruhig.*" Quiet. Thor maintained his fierce posture but dropped the snarl.

"*Gute Hund.*" Good dog, Linda countered the command.

Thor looked up at her and wagged his tail happily. She tossed him a doggie treat, which he caught midair and crunched happily.

She didn't bother looking up at Jurgen as she knelt once more to check over the little dog. His scruffy fur was so soft that it tickled. Good strength in the jaw, enough to show he'd had bite training despite his size —perfect if she ever needed to take down a three-foot-tall terrorist. Legs said he was a jumper.

"Take your time, Hamlin. I've got nothing else to do

with the rest of my goddamn day except babysit you and this mutt."

"Is the course set?"

"Sure. Take him out," Jurgen's snarl sounded almost as nasty as Thor's before he stalked off.

She stood and slapped a hand on her opposite shoulder.

Thor sprang aloft as if he was attached to springs and she caught him easily. He'd cleared well over double his own height. Definitely trained...and far easier to catch than seventy pounds of hyperactive Malinois.

She plopped him back down on the ground. On lead or off? She'd give him the benefit of the doubt and try off first to see what happened.

Linda zipped up her brand-new USSS jacket against the cold and led the way out of the kennel into the hard sunlight of the January morning. Snow had brushed the higher hills around the USSS James J. Rowley Training Center—which this close to Washington, DC, wasn't saying much—but was melting quickly. Scents wouldn't carry as well on the cool air, making it more of a challenge for Thor to locate the explosives. She didn't know where they were either. The course was a test for handler as well as dog.

Jurgen would be up in the observer turret looking for any excuse to mark down his newest team. Perhaps teasing him about being just a Marine hadn't been her best tactical choice. She sighed. At least she was consistent—she'd always been good at finding ways to piss people off before she could stop herself and consider the wisdom of doing so.

This test was the culmination of a crazy three months, so she'd forgive herself this time—something she also wasn't very good at.

In October she'd been out of the Army and unsure what to do next. Tucked in the packet with her DD 214 honorable discharge form had been a flyer on career opportunities with the US Secret Service dog team: *Be all your dog can be!* No one else being released from Fort Benning that day had received any kind of a job flyer at all that she'd seen, so she kept quiet about it.

She had to pass through DC on her way back to Vermont—her parent's place. Burlington would work for, honestly, not very long at all, but she lacked anywhere else to go after a decade of service. So, she'd stopped off in DC to see what was up with that job flyer. Five interviews and three months to complete a standard six-month training course later—which was mostly a cakewalk after fighting with the US Rangers —she was on-board and this chill January day was her first chance with a dog. First chance to prove that she still had it. First chance to prove that she hadn't made a mistake in deciding that she'd seen enough bloodshed and war zones for one lifetime and leaving the Army.

The Start Here sign made it obvious where to begin, but she didn't dare hesitate to take in her surroundings past a quick glimpse. Jurgen's score would count a great deal toward where she and Thor were assigned in the future. Mostly likely on some field prep team, clearing the way for presidential visits.

As usual, hindsight informed her that harassing the lieutenant hadn't been an optimal strategy. A hindsight that had served her equally poorly with regular Army commanders before she'd finally hooked up with the Rangers—kowtowing to officers had never been one of her strengths.

Thankfully, the Special Operations Forces hadn't given a damn about anything except performance and *that* she could always deliver, since the day she'd been named the team captain for both soccer and volleyball. She was never popular, but both teams had made all-state her last two years in school.

The canine training course at James J. Rowley was a two-acre lot. A hard-packed path of tramped-down dirt led through the brown grass. It followed a predictable pattern from the gate to a junker car, over to tool shed, then a truck, and so on into a compressed version of an intersection in a small town. Beyond it ran an urban street of gray clapboard two- and three-story buildings and an eight-story office tower, all without windows. Clearly a playground for Secret Service training teams.

Her target was the town, so she blocked the city street out of her mind. Focus on the problem: two roads, twenty storefronts, six houses, vehicles, pedestrians.

It might look normal...normalish with its missing windows and no movement. It would be anything but. Stocked with fake IEDs, a bombmaker's stash, suicide cars, weapons caches, and dozens of other traps, all waiting for her and Thor to find. He had to be sensitive to hundreds of scents and it was her job to guide him so that he didn't miss the opportunity to find and evaluate each one.

There would be easy scents, from fertilizer and diesel fuel used so destructively in the 1995 Oklahoma City bombing, to almost as obvious TNT to the very difficult to detect C-4 plastic explosive.

Mannequins on the street carried grocery bags and briefcases. Some held fresh meat, a powerful smell demanding any dog's attention, but would count as a false lead if they went for it. On the job, an explosives detection dog wasn't supposed to care about anything except explosives. Other mannequins were wrapped in suicide vests loaded with Semtex or wearing knapsacks filled with package bombs made from Russian PVV-5A.

She spotted Jurgen stepping into a glassed-in observer turret atop the corner drugstore. Someone else was already there and watching.

She looked down once more at the ridiculous little dog and could only hope for the best.

"Thor?"

He looked up at her.

She pointed to the left, away from the beaten path.

"Such!" Find.

Thor sniffed left, then right. Then he headed forward quickly in the direction she pointed.

———

Clive Andrews sat in the second-story window at the corner of Main and First, the only two streets in town. Downstairs was a drugstore all rigged to explode, except there were no triggers and there was barely enough explosive to blow up a candy box.

Not that he'd know, but that's what Lieutenant Jurgen had promised him.

It didn't really matter if it was rigged to blow for real, because when Miss Watson—never Ms. or Mrs.—asked for a "favor," you did it. At least he did. Actually, he had yet to meet anyone else who knew her. Not that he'd asked around. She wasn't the sort of person one talked about with strangers, or even close friends. He'd bet even if they did, it would be in whispers. That's just what she was like.

So he'd traveled across town from the White House and into Maryland on a cold winter's morning, barely past a sunrise that did nothing to warm the day. Now he sat in an unheated glass icebox and watched a new officer run a test course he didn't begin to understand. Lieutenant Jurgen settled in beside him at a console with feeds from a dozen cameras and banks of switches.

While waiting, Clive had been fooling around with a sketch on a small pad of paper. The next State Dinner was in seven days. President Zachary Taylor had invited the leaders of Vietnam, Japan, and the Philippines to the White House for discussions about some Chinese islands. Or something like that, Clive hadn't really been paying attention to the details past the attendee list.

Instead, he was contemplating the dessert for such a dinner that would surprise, perhaps delight, as well as being an icebreaker for future discussions. Being the chocolatier for the White House was the most exciting job he'd ever had. Every challenge was fresh and new, like the first strawberry of each year.

This one would be elegant. January was a little early, it would be better if it was spring, but that wasn't crucial. A large half-egg shape of paper-thin white chocolate filled with a mousse—white chocolate? No, nor a dark chocolate. Instead, a milk chocolate mousse but rich with flavor, perhaps bourbon. Then mold the dark chocolate to top it with a filigree bird, wings spread in half flight, ready to soar upward. A crane perhaps? He made a note to check with the protocol office to make sure that he wouldn't be offending some leader without knowing it.

"Never underestimate the power of a good dessert," he mumbled one of Jacques Torres' favorite admonitions. This was going to work very nicely.

"What's that?" Jurgen grunted out without looking up.

"Just talking to myself."

Which earned him a dismissive grunt, as if he was unworthy of the agent's attention. It wouldn't surprise him.

———

Keep reading now!
Available at fine retailers everywhere.
Off the Leash

ABOUT THE AUTHOR

USA Today and Amazon #1 Bestseller M. L. "Matt" Buchman started writing on a flight south from Japan to ride his bicycle across the Australian Outback. Just part of a solo around-the-world trip that ultimately launched his writing career.

From the very beginning, his powerful female heroines insisted on putting character first, *then* a great adventure. He's since written over 60 action-adventure thrillers and military romantic suspense novels. And just for the fun of it: 100 short stories, and a fast-growing pile of read-by-author audiobooks.

Booklist says: "3X Top 10 of the Year." PW says: "Tom Clancy fans open to a strong female lead will clamor for more." His fans say: "I want more now...of everything." That his characters are even more insistent than his fans is a hoot.

As a 30-year project manager with a geophysics degree who has designed and built houses, flown and jumped out of planes, and solo-sailed a 50' ketch, he is awed by what is possible. More at: www. mlbuchman.com.

Other works by M. L. Buchman: *(* - also in audio)*

Other works by M. L. Buchman:

Contemporary Romance (cont)

Love Abroad
Heart of the Cotswolds: England
Path of Love: Cinque Terre, Italy

Where Dreams
Where Dreams are Born
Where Dreams Reside
Where Dreams Are of Christmas*
Where Dreams Unfold
Where Dreams Are Written

Science Fiction / Fantasy

Deities Anonymous
Cookbook from Hell: Reheated
Saviors 101

Single Titles
The Nara Reaction
Monk's Maze
the Me and Elsie Chronicles

Non-Fiction

Strategies for Success
Managing Your Inner Artist/Writer
Estate Planning for Authors*
Character Voice
Narrate and Record Your Own
Audiobook*

Short Story Series by M. L. Buchman:

Romantic Suspense

Delta Force
Th Delta Force Shooters
The Delta Force Warriors

Firehawks
The Firehawks Lookouts
The Firehawks Hotshots
The Firebirds

The Night Stalkers
The Night Stalkers 5D Stories
The Night Stalkers 5E Stories
The Night Stalkers CSAR
The Night Stalkers Wedding Stories

US Coast Guard

White House Protection Force

Contemporary Romance

Eagle Cove

Henderson's Ranch*

Where Dreams

Action-Adventure Thrillers

Dead Chef

Miranda Chase Origin Stories

Science Fiction / Fantasy

Deities Anonymous

Other
The Future Night Stalkers
Single Titles

SIGN UP FOR M. L. BUCHMAN'S NEWSLETTER TODAY

and receive:
Release News
Free Short Stories
a Free Book

Get your free book today. Do it now.
free-book.mlbuchman.com

www.ingramcontent.com/pod-product-compliance
Lightning Source LLC
Chambersburg PA
CBHW020634130626
46552CB00003B/1219